Ceri & Deri – Get Your Skates On
Published in Great Britain in 2021 by Graffeg
Limited.

Written and illustrated by Max Low
copyright © 2021. Designed and produced by
Graffeg Limited copyright © 2021.

Graffeg Limited, 24 Stradey Park Business
Centre, Mwrwg Road, Llangennech, Llanelli,
Carmarthenshire, SA14 8YP, Wales, UK.
Tel: 01554 824000. www.graffeg.com.

A CIP Catalogue record for this book is available
from the British Library.

ISBN 9781913134501

1 2 3 4 5 6 7 8 9

Ceri & Deri

GET YOUR SKATES ON

written and
illustrated
by
MAX LOW

GRAFFEG

Ceri is a cat. Deri is a dog.

Ceri has stripes and Deri has spots.

They live in a small town by a big hill near a small mountain and they do everything together.

They are best friends.

Ceri and Deri are at the skatepark.

Dai the duck was a bit too nervous to go on his own, so Ceri and Deri went with him.

That's the kind of stuff friends do.

Dai falls over.

'OUCH!' he says. 'This is embarrassing, I'm not as good as this lot. Look at Barbara the Bear! I'll never be a cool bear and be called Barbara and be awesome.'

'Don't be daft, you dafty duck!' says Ceri as they help him up. 'You've just got to practise some more.'

'No, I give up, let's just play a quiz or something. I am super smart and stuff,' says Dai.

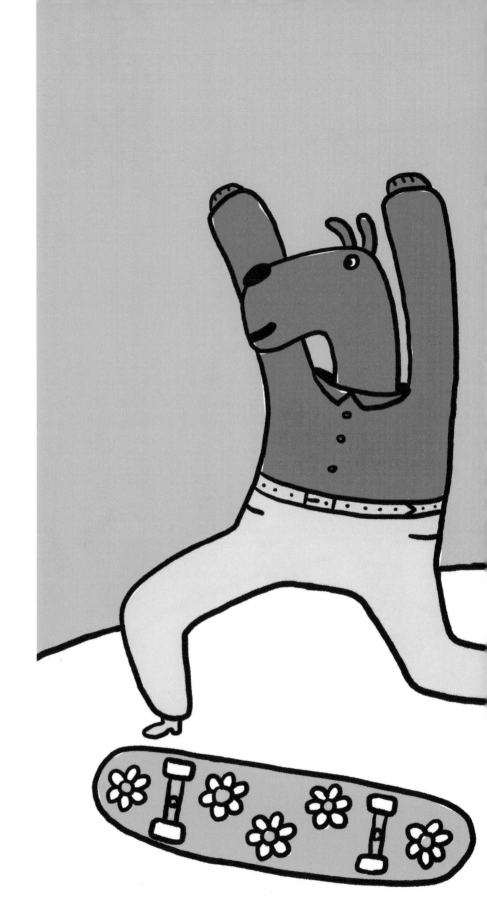

'Ok, Dai, spell rhinoceros!' asks Deri.

'Right, I got this... R... I... N... O... S... A... R... U... S.'

'Um... sounds right to me!' says Deri.

Unfortunately, Ceri and Deri have no idea how to spell rhinoceros either.

'YES! I AM SO SMART!' shouts Dai.

'Oh, excuse me,' says a passing rhinoceros.
'I think you'll find it's spelt R-H-I-N-O-C-E-R-O-S.'

'Hah! No chance! That's silly! How would you know anyway?!' says Dai, laughing.

'Because, my dear sir, I AM a RHINOCEROS.'

'He's got a point there, Dai,' says Ceri.

'Well, maybe I'm pants at spelling,' says Dai, 'but you don't need to be good at spelling to be a... ROCKSTAR, OH YEAHHH! I have always wanted to be a rockstar! Let's form a band!'

So Ceri finds some bins to bang on and keep the rhythm.

Deri grabs an old tennis racket and makes guitar noises, *badowng badowng*.

Dai finds an old keyboard and jumps on the keys while singing, 'We are a hefty metal band, with hefty metal plans, and if you think that we are cool, that's because we are beautiful.'

'WILL YOU LOT PIPE DOWN!'
shouts a punk rock dude out of
his window. 'I'm trying to watch
In Praise of Antiques on the
telly!'

'Oooh, you know what an awesome character like me would be good at... Inventing things!' suggests Dai.

So they go to Ceri's workshop, where she fixes stuff. Dai bangs and clangs for a while before presenting them with his new invention.

'LOOK AT THIS, WOW! It's a seat for your bum so you can sit down when you're working at your desk! I call it... the bum seat!' explains Dai excitedly.

'Oh cool, like a chair?' says Deri. 'You're standing on one right now.'

'Hmm... maybe I should give rugby a go, since I am SO strong,' says Dai.

Unfortunately for Dai, he quickly gets mistaken for a rugby ball and Ceri and Deri have to run onto the pitch to save him from being launched through the big H!

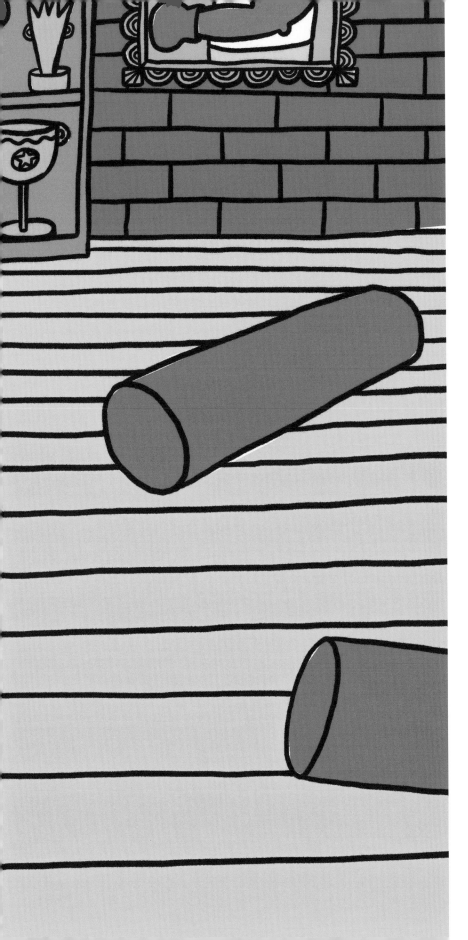

'Ugh, perhaps I am not best suited to a sport of such brutality... What about boxing?' says Dai.

So they go to Tuff Tammy's Boxing Palace, where Tuff Tammy thumps the competition!

'Boxing is about discipline and respect, Dai,' she says as he punches her ankles. 'I think that you should return when you're a little older.'

'You know, maybe I am not the sporting type. I could just picture myself in a fancy coffee house, discussing philosophy and writing poetry. Don't you agree, my chapalaps?' says Dai in his most refined accent.

'Yep, absolutely, matey boy!' Ceri and Deri reply.

Dai slurps his coffee in the most elegant manner a duck could possibly slurp coffee.

'Listen to my new poem on the futility of existence... it's entitled The Cobweb.

Oh cobweb that hangs in my bathroom,

I am a duck! I am not your prey,

You catch me again in your shroud of doom,

I wish that you would go, go away.'

Ceri and Deri clap politely.

'It's no good. I might be a poetic GENIUS, but all I want to do is skateboard! But I'm the worst at it!' says Dai, and walks back home.

Ceri and Deri don't know what to do, but they have a think and come up with an idea.

The next morning, Dai wakes up to the sound of clattering wheels. It's Ceri and Deri, with someone else... Barbara the Bear!

'Hey, Dai, let's go skateboarding!' she calls out.

'Wow, I would love to, Barbara the Bear, but I'm not very good at it... in fact, I'm really kind of poopy at it!'

'I'm only good at skating because I've fallen over so much,' explains Barbara. 'Every time I fall over, I get back up and try again. And every time I try again, I fall over a bit less! I only really do it because I get to hang out with my friends and have fun... otherwise, what's the point?'

Dai decided to continue to do what he loved, no matter how good he was at it, and pretty soon he was zooming around the skatepark with all his friends.

Ceri & Deri

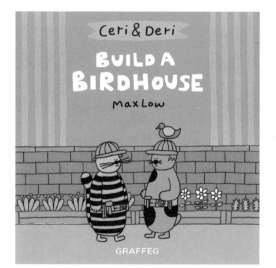